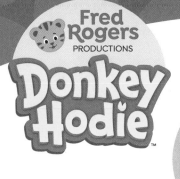

The Missing Notebook!

adapted by **Tina Gallo**

based on the screenplay "Poetry Problem"

written by **Louie Lazar and Stephanie D'Abruzzo**

Ready-to-Read

Simon Spotlight

New York   London   Toronto   Sydney   New Delhi

SIMON SPOTLIGHT

An imprint of Simon & Schuster Children's Publishing Division

1230 Avenue of the Americas, New York, New York 10020

This Simon Spotlight edition December 2022

© 2022 The Fred Rogers Company.

Donkey Hodie is produced by Fred Rogers Productions and Spiffy Pictures.

All rights reserved, including the right of reproduction in whole or in part in any form.

SIMON SPOTLIGHT, READY-TO-READ, and colophon are registered trademarks of Simon & Schuster, Inc.

For information about special discounts for bulk purchases, please contact Simon & Schuster Special Sales at 1-866-506-1949 or business@simonandschuster.com.

Manufactured in the United States of America 1122 LAK

10 9 8 7 6 5 4 3 2 1

ISBN 978-1-6659-2835-9 (hc)

ISBN 978-1-6659-2834-2 (pbk)

ISBN 978-1-6659-2836-6 (ebook)

Donkey Hodie
woke up smiling.
"That dance party with
Purple Panda last night
was so much fun!"
she said.

"But this place sure
is messy," she said.

Donkey knew she had to clean up the mess.

"You can do this,
Donkey Hodie,"
she said.

"It's cleanup time!"

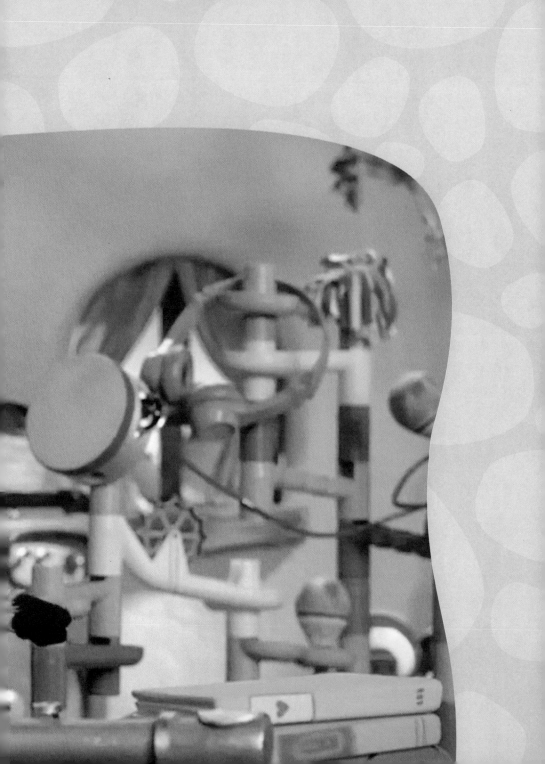

Just then her best friend,
Purple Panda, called from
the Planet Purple
Poetry Recital.

He wanted to read a poem
he had written.

But there was a problem.
"I left my poetry notebook
at your house!"
Panda said.

"Not to worry, purple pal.
I, Donkey Hodie,
will find your notebook!"
she told him.

"And then I will read
the poem to you. And you
will be able to read it
to all the pandas!"

But Donkey could not
find the notebook anywhere
in her messy living room.

"Think, Donkey Hodie, think!
I know I have to clean up.
But cleaning is no fun!"
she said.

Then Donkey found
her maracas.
"Hey! Maybe I can make
cleaning fun!"

"Making music while I am cleaning is hee-hawesome!" she cheered.

Donkey played music and sang while she cleaned.

"Hee-haw! Clean up!

It can be fun. Oh yes it can!

Hee-haw! Clean up!

Having fun till I'm done.

Yes, that's the plan!"

Soon the room was clean.
But Donkey still
had not found
the notebook.

"I still have two rooms left to clean," Donkey said. "How can I make cleaning the kitchen fun?"

"I know! I will be a superhero!" she exclaimed. "With this costume on, I can handle any kitchen mess!"

"Hee-haw! Clean up!
It can be fun. Oh yes it can!
Hee-haw! Clean up!
Having fun till I'm done.
Yes, that's the plan!"

Soon the kitchen was clean.
And Donkey had fun
cleaning!
But she had still not found
the notebook.

Finally, it was time to clean her bedroom.

Donkey knew just what to do.

Donkey turned cleaning her room into a fun game of trunkball.

"Swish!" she cheered,
as she tossed costumes
into the trunk.

Soon Donkey found the notebook!

She called Panda.

He was thrilled!

Donkey read him his poem.

Then, Panda read the poem
to the purple pandas.
They loved it!

"Thank you, Donkey!"
Panda said.

"You're welcome,
my favorite purple poet!"
said Donkey.